THE CURSED FROG
AND
OTHER MODERN FAIRY TALES
FOR GROWN-UPS

Jason Antoon

DUTCH KILLS PRESS
NEW YORK

For Seana and the HaHa's

Contents

The Horn Breaker

A retired ballet dancer named Ann awoke in the early hours of the New Year to a commercial on her video screen. A handsome television host promised to rid anyone of their demons. "The Horn Breakers will fight for you and your loved ones," he said. "No prescriptions. No therapy. No exorcists needed."

Her whole life Ann had battled her inner demons, and she was losing. Now she found that she had a new purpose. So she headed to the office of The Horn Breakers, a custom vintage van decorated with a psychedelic airbrush of a silhouetted figure wielding a flaming sword surrounded by ominous yellow fog. Above the image, in a trippy font, it read: *The Horn Breakers.* At first, Ann was hesitant to knock, as warnings from her childhood reminded her that only bad things happen inside "shaggin' wagons." But knock she did, and when the side door slid open she was greeted not by the handsome TV host, but by an ugly, squat imp with a ruby tooth. For such a small man he looked strong and battle-worn. He wore earbuds that dangled to a device in one of the many pockets on his overalls.

"Can I help you?" he said.

"I need to clear myself of my demons," Ann said, trying not to eye the carpeted interior behind the three foot man.

"You came to the wrong place. We don't 'clear' here, we kill. Literally."

"I don't care what you call it. I just want my life back."

"Come inside. We'll discuss the details," the imp said.

For some reason Ann knew she'd be safe inside the van. They sat on the shag carpeting.

"Do you have an item from your childhood? Something you cherished?"

"There's a talking doll my parents got me for my sixth birthday. It's in a box somewhere in my attic."

"Very well. Fill out this contract, and if you can afford our services, we can get started immediately."

Of course she could afford it. The imp's lack of culture meant that he did not recognize Ann as the former prima ballerina of the New York City Ballet. She was famously known as the "bipolar ballerina" because no one performance was the same, and one was lucky enough to be in attendance on a night she had a manic episode. But an injury befell her when a set piece collapsed onto her ankle, winning her a hefty settlement and forcing her into retirement.

As the imp looked over the contract, he was deeply concerned. He hadn't yet dealt with a demon as powerful as what she claimed.

"I implore you to find that doll," the imp said. "We will need to bring it with us."

"Bring it where?" Ann asked.

"You'll see," the imp said.

Ann drove home, ran up to her attic and found the doll. On its ratty houndstooth dress was the doll's name: *Beulah*. She pulled the doll's string, but its voice box wasn't operating.

The next day Ann and her doll were back at the Horn Breakers office, seated on the shag carpet, across from the imp. After payment was verified, he unzipped a leather medicine bag and took out a large handheld mirror.

The imp said, "Would you mind looking at my mirror, Ann?"

He lifted the mirror and faced it and held it up behind him so that the two of them were framed inside its milky surface.

"I need you to think of the person who did you harm all those years ago. Call out to the monster, and it will come."

The imp held up the mirror for as long as Ann needed. She was clearly struggling to even utter its name.

"Ch...char..." Ann mumbled.

"Louder. It needs to hear you," the imp said.

"I can't," Ann said.

"I know it's hard, but try and reach deep down and open those floodgates. *Say his name!*"

Ann's body quivered with such ferociousness that when the demon's name came out it sounded like a pained primal scream:

"*Charles!*"

A sinister-looking yellow fog streamed from the mirror into the van. As it filled the interior, Ann noticed her surroundings alter into a disorienting endless shadowed dreamscape. Suddenly a face appeared in the mirror, a demon with black horns. Ann jolted and screamed as the demon lept from the mirror to tower over her. Strings of saliva dripped from its jagged teeth onto her face.

"I remember you," the demon said.

Before he could say anything more a ringing was heard from behind the beast. A flaming sword came down on one of the demon's black horns, severing it at the base. The imp, bloodied sword in hand, stood confidently in front of Ann. The wounded and now one-horned demon struggled to its feet and ran off in a howl.

The imp adjusted his earbuds.

Ann looked up at the ugly imp.

"Is that it?" she asked. "Are we done?"

"Oh no, no, no, that was just the beginning. We must go find it and you must kill it for good. For only you can kill your own demon. But it won't be easy. Charles has had years to grow and become strong. But we know what he looks like now. Come. We will need to get you a weapon."

Ann followed the imp through the yellow fog. The fog was dotted with small red eyes, and there were horrible noises, screams and distant calls for help. A cold wind whipped up as a mountain came into view.

"We'll need to cross that mountain to get to the armorist," the imp said. "He will know what to make you, Ann."

Demons of all shapes and sizes were everywhere — formless demons created from the painful psyches of their victims, fat and greedy demons feeding on the memories of the ones they abused. Some were so tall you couldn't see their eyes above the yellow fog. Others covered the bodies of their victims in a dreadful skin suit. But they didn't pay much attention to Ann as she passed. She wasn't their problem.

It was a longer journey to the armorist than Ann had expected. They passed other people like her, those who had come to fight their demons, some successful, others not so lucky. They watched two young boys battling their demon with focused anger, but the demon impaled them both with each sharp horn. The demon tossed the limp bodies of the boys aside and then drifted cackling into the void of the yellow fog.

"I told those kids to hire me," the imp said. "But they didn't listen. They went with a cheaper horn breaker. It's like in your world. There are good shamans and bad shamans. There are quality headphones on Amazon and there are knockoffs. Never go with the knockoff."

The imp pushed his earbuds tightly into place.

To take her mind away from her fear, Ann asked the imp what he was listening to.

"If you must know," the imp said, "I am listening to the soothing sounds of Yanni and his world music."

The path to the armorist was unimpeded and Ann, with the aid of the imp, was able to continue the journey. But something nagged at her.

"Does it all have to be so violent?" she asked the imp. "Isn't there a peaceful way to do this?"

"Violence has a hundred percent success rate."

"Have you tried another way?"

"Why would I? When you kill your demon," the imp explained, "you are ridding yourself of the trauma you have lived with. But the memory will always remain. It's all in the contract's fine print."

When they reached the armorist, the imp greeted him with little fanfare, as if they had been colleagues for years. The armorist happened to be the handsome television host that had caused Ann to hire Horn Breakers in the first place. The imp whispered Ann's dilemma in the armorist's ear; the armorist nodded.

"She needs a sword," the armorist said.

"I don't want a sword," Ann said. "I need you to repair Beulah. She's lost her voice."

"This is a place for swords, my dear," the imp scoffed, shuffling through his new Enya playlist. "Not dolls."

"Maybe we can compromise," the armorist said.

The armorist stoked his furnace and hammered away at his anvil. Finally he dipped the new sword into a deep pail of water, creating a cloud of steam. He asked Ann to approach the sword and to place her hand on its hilt. At first Ann was afraid, but when she wrapped her fingers around the grip she saw that Beulah the doll was fashioned to the crossguard of the sword, like a figurehead on a ship. Ann raised the weapon and felt powerful, rejuvenated. She pulled on Beulah's string.

"Hi!", the doll said in a clear cute voice. "I've missed you ever so much."

"You're making a mistake with that doll," the imp said.

It was Beulah who led the way to Charles, pointing this way and that with her little doll hand, smiling at its newfound life. They reached the demon's cave, and Ann rested the point of her new sword on the ground. She felt alive.

"Charles!" she yelled. "Please come out!"

"You must get *angry*, dear," the imp warned. "This soft method will get you killed."

The one-horned demon slowly walked out of its cave, head down, toward Ann. Something was different about it.

"Ann, listen to me," it said. "This is not just my fault. Your mother allowed me to do those things. She turned a blind eye. She could have stopped me. And who paid for all those ballet lessons when you were little? Me. I did."

"Don't listen," the imp said. "It's a trick."

The demon took a step back, its face scrunched. It was afraid of something Ann held. It wasn't her sword. It was the doll attached to it.

"Where did you get that?"

"Oh, so you remember Beulah. Good, because she remembers everything." Ann pulled the doll's string again.

"Hi," the doll said, waving adorably at the demon. "Would you like to tell me a secret?"

The demon let out a mind-splitting roar. It charged at Ann, who at the last second gracefully leapt out of the way. The imp deftly stepped between them and easily countered the demon's next attack with his own sword, his earbuds popping out. For a moment it looked like the imp would be victorious, but as he was re-inserting his ear buds the demon swung its tail around, tripping up the imp. The demon rose and jumped with all his might. It slammed down upon the imp's face with its heavy hooves, flattening his skull. As Ann stood shocked and saddened she could faintly hear the music of Tangerine Dream coming from his dislodged ear buds.

The demon laughed. He pushed Ann to the ground and squatted over her splayed body.

"Just like old times, sweetie," the demon said.

The doll said, "Sometimes it's okay to apologize to the ones you hurt."

The demon began to sniff Ann.

"Would you like to say sorry?" asked the doll.

The demon licked its lips.

"Remember to lay still and keep quiet, Ann," he whispered. "Be a good girl."

"We think you've said enough!" Beulah exclaimed. "Now fuck off."

Beulah reached out her two small doll hands and pulled out the demon's wriggling tongue, showering blood on both of them.

The demon let out a terrible cry and bit into the doll's body, tearing it from the sword's hilt and tossing it aside, next to its own twitching severed tongue.

Ann was now alone to face her demon. She was afraid. But then Charles lowered his massive body down to the cold ground. It dropped his head from exhaustion, blood oozing from his mouth. It tried to speak but could only produce an awful gurgling sound.

Ann felt pity for Charles.

She placed the imp's ear buds into her ears and scrolled through his song list. She stopped on The Cocteau Twins and clicked on the song "Carolyn's Fingers."

Ann stood up and danced. She let the music dictate her performance and lost herself in a trance. From plié, she relevéd in fifth. An Arabesque led to a grand pas de chat. Her moves were effortless, graceful. As she performed in front of Charles, she pirouetted, raising her sword high. She leapt at Charles with a perfect grand jeté and as she landed she sliced off his remaining horn and then drove her sword deep into its skull.

The demon was killed.

Months later, Ann felt better with each passing day. Every week Ann, with her newly stitched-up Beulah, drove the vintage van to meet new clients who needed help with their own demons. From her rear-view mirror, the imp's earbuds dangled and swayed. A pair of horns prominently placed as the van's hood ornament reminded Ann, and everyone who cared, of her new life as a horn breaker.

The Actor

Once upon a time there was an actor who had two percent body fat and a face that redefined the word "beauty." One critic boldly stated that looking at his piercing blue eyes was like looking into God's. When his agent advised him to start a Twitter account, his followers went from zero to one million in a day. Once daily the actor snapped a smiling photo of himself, either with his shirt off or lounging in a hammock made of organic hemp. Then he would Instagram it with a nice Amaro filter and Tweet it.

The actor spent all day Tweeting on his phone. He was on his phone at the coffee joint, in the gym, on the toilet, and even while driving. He had to tell his followers everything he was doing, and they loved it.

Soon he had over two million followers. He would say to his reflection, "Two million." His reflection smiled back, and he liked that. He liked how he looked in car mirrors and in storefront windows and passing hallway mirrors and shiny toasters and other people's sunglasses. He liked himself so much that he started another Twitter account just so he could follow his official verified account and dialogue with it.

One day his agent called and said there was this woman who wanted to pay him to come to her daughter's eighteenth birthday celebration. The actor couldn't say no to one of his biggest fans—and her mother's offer of two hundred thousand dollars. But there was a twist. This woman wanted the actor to impregnate her daughter. The woman guaranteed that if the actor did impregnate her daughter, he would never grow old, never age and never lose his fame or his Twitter followers. The actor looked at his reflection in the mirror of a Starbucks bathroom and thought about it. Suddenly his reflection berated the actor for even considering the offer.

"This is a bad idea," said his reflection. "I don't trust that woman."

The actor frowned. He was in some kind of rock-and-hard-place situation and he didn't like it. Things usually came easy to him in life.

So he went to his Twitter account and asked his followers

what he should do. An avalanche of suggestions filled his inbox—so many that he had to hire an assistant to read them all to him while he rocked gently in his hammock of organic hemp. Half his followers wanted him to listen to his reflection and half wanted him to impregnate the lucky eighteen-year-old girl and Instagram it. Now he was really confused. He thanked all his followers by tweeting a semi-nude pic of himself standing on his rooftop.

As the big day came upon him, the actor decided that it was in his best interests to attend the eighteenth birthday, receive the two hundred thousand dollars and impregnate the women's daughter. It wasn't like he had to be a hands-on father. And he'd retain his good looks and his millions of followers. What could possibly go wrong, he said to the reflection of himself in a shiny spoon.

"Please don't do this," said the reflection. "You still have time to leave. I don't trust that witchy woman."

"Witch?" asked the actor.

"The woman is a witch and so is her daughter."

"There's no such thing as witches," said the actor to his reflection. He ended the conversation by plunging the spoon deep in his non-GMO strawberry sorbet.

The actor was a big hit at the party and all the birthday girl's friends were jealous that she was going to be impregnated by the famous actor with eyes like God's.

After the cake, it was time for the actor to take the birthday girl to her bedroom. As her mother escorted them down the hall, she gave the actor a breath mint.

"Kiss her first, that's all I ask," said the mother with a twinkle in her eye. Behind her the actor's reflection in the glass covering a Miro painting was waving his hands frantically to get his attention. The actor ignored his reflection and followed the birthday girl into the bedroom.

The actor and the birthday girl copulated for three strenuous hours. At first the actor thought he was falling in love, but then he felt his body turning cold. The birthday girl made sure that the actor shot his seed inside her. And then he turned to stone.

Ten years later a little boy with god-like eyes passed by the statue in the hall of mirrors, his mother by his side.

"Mommy, who's that?" he asked.

"That was mommy's birthday present when she was eighteen."

"Will I get a present like that one day?"

"Maybe. If you wish hard enough."

They walked away, leaving the statue of the actor forever standing, never aging, never getting old.

The statue's official Twitter account now has 35 million followers.

The Rich Lady's House

High in the hills above the crowded streets of the flatlands lived a forty-something single woman who had more money than God. She hadn't earned this money; she had inherited it the day she was born. And if she ever has children, their children's children will still have more money than God, even if He invested wisely.

Her home was like a castle atop a pointy peak surrounded by two sets of gates. She loved throwing dinner parties and brunches. All her friends would come over weekly and liven up her life with conversations about politics or the latest celebrity breakup. As the years passed, her friends started to realize that their friend at the top of the tallest hill never ventured out from her property.

She didn't want to. She didn't need to. Everything she ever wanted or needed was in her house or could be delivered at any time. There is a cost to everything and she could cover it. She had no man or woman in her life, just her groundskeeper, whom she called Taquito. She liked him because he was friendly and always wore a smile. But mainly she liked him because through him she felt in touch with the poor and dirty people in the flatlands way, way below her house. And Taquito made her garden look lush and beautiful.

One day, Taquito knocked on her back door. She had fourteen back doors, but he always knew which one she would be closest to. When she answered she was surprised to see that it was raining and that Taquito was soaked to the bone. She did not invite him in.

"How long has it been raining?" she asked Taquito.

"Three weeks, ma'am," he said, noticing crumbs of all sorts on her silk robe, most likely bits of Pringles and chocolate nibs and a few kernels of brown rice.

"What seems to be the problem, Taquito?"

"Well ma'am, I was cleaning the weeds around the foundation and I noticed that all this rain is causing your house to sink and lean a little."

"Lean which way?"

"Towards the cliff."

She gasped and slammed the door in Taquito's face. But then opened it again and threw a towel at him. "Dry off. Then go to Home Depot and get a bus full of your kind and bring them back here at once," she said. "Here is a cold coconut water for you to enjoy on the way."

Taquito hated coconut water. Nevertheless he went to Home Dept and returned with a busload of his "kind." He knocked on the back door.

"I have done what you said, ma'am," he told her.

She glanced behind him and saw the workers standing in the pouring rain.

"Good," she said, "Now here's what I want them to do. Place them around the house, spread them out equally, and have them brace the walls so the house won't fall down the hill."

Taquito and his men did as she told them. But the rain never stopped. It fell harder and harder. The house began to tip even more now. The rich lady sent Taquito back down to the Home Depot to bring more men. The men were earning good money so they did as she requested, without protest or emotion. Nevertheless Taquito felt that he should warn the rich lady that if she didn't leave her home, it would fall down the cliff and she would fall with it.

"Ma'am, your money won't save you," he said.

"If I wanted your opinion Taquito," she replied, stone-faced, "I would pay you for it. Now go get more men. *Vamanos!*"

After five weeks of unrelenting rain she threw a dinner party and all her friends came over. They didn't question why her house was leaning toward the cliff and why there were so many dark-skinned men circling her house. They ate the pâté and drank the expensive wines. When it was late, they all left and carefully drove back down to the bustling, soaked flatlands.

But blocking their path was a huge castle-like house scattered all over the flatlands. Five dozen dark-skinned men lay dead. When the authorities finally cleaned up the mess there was no trace of the rich lady's body. They did find her personal safe. It was about the size of a school bus. They pried it open to reveal the rich lady inside, a little shaken up, but safe and sound and surrounded and cushioned by all her money.

The Time Cheater

A man named Job, who worked for a company called the Time Traveling Courier Agency (TTCA), had finished up a day of delivering care packages to various people in the 19th century. He himself traveled through time in a Victorian-era wooden crib. Before he headed back to 2021, he stopped off in 1992 at a young girl named Betsy's apartment to have a few hours of sex-fueled fun. On his way out, he pocketed a pair of her pink underwear and headed forward to the present time.

He arrived home to find Betsy again waiting for him, but now looking older and a lot less sexy. She held their baby and demanded to know why he was so late. Too tired to answer, he took the baby in his arms. As Betsy repeated her demand for an explanation, the baby put his curious hand into his daddy's pocket and retrieved the pink underwear.

Betsy grabbed them.

"Whose are these?"

"They're yours," Job said.

"I haven't worn a size two since college. Oh my God, you're having an affair."

"It's not what you think, babe."

"Who is she?"

Job explained delicately to Betsy that between his TTCA assignments he had been traveling back to 1992 to "hang out" with her younger self.

"So you are cheating on me!"

"If it's still you, then how can it be cheating?"

"Fuck you! I'm a completely different person than I was back then."

"And much more fun to be with I might add."

With that she slapped him in the face.

The baby started crying.

"It's okay," Job said to the baby. "I'm sorry, but I don't see the problem here," he said to his wife.

Betsy was pacing the room frantically.

"Oh my god, this is my biggest fear. That you'd want someone younger than me. And it's *me*."

"Calm down, Betsy."

"I want to meet her."

"What?"

Betsy grabbed the baby and climbed into the Victorian crib. She pressed some buttons and the crib began to undulate. Job dove into the crib at the last second.

The crib and its occupants blinked into a small studio apartment, startling a woman on a couch—a young Betsy, who was reading the latest Tom Robbins novel. Old Betsy climbed out and sat by Young Betsy, who smiled when she saw the baby, understanding immediately that it was her future child.

"I'm so sorry," Young Betsy said to Old Betsy, "I didn't know he was married, let alone married to my future self."

"When you get older you'll get better at spotting assholes," Old Betsy said.

"You guys are making a huge deal out of nothing," Job said from the crib.

"Listen," Old Betsy said to Young Betsy. "You'll meet a guy at a jazz club later this week, a bass player. I always regretted not sleeping with him. Will you do that for me? For us, I mean?"

"Of course," Young Betsy said, nodding. "But what's it like for us later in life, did we accomplish everything we dreamed of?"

Old Betsy thought for a moment.

"Have sex with that bass player," she said. "And go on that trip to New Zealand. Don't settle down, and buy that apartment five years from now. You hear me?"

As they hugged, the crib began to undulate and vibrate. Before Old Betsy could lunge for the railing, it vanished with Job inside.

"Son of a bitch!" wailed Old Betsy.

"Now what?" asked Young Betsy.

Days later, in Pittsburgh, Pennsylvania, Old Betsy, now stuck in the past forever, knocked on a dorm room door. A young man opened the door, holding a smoking blue bong—Job, when he was not yet an asshole and still cute.

"Can I help you?"

"You can," Betsy said. "I am your future wife, and this is your future child."

She handed Young Job their baby and walked into the dorm room to start their new life.

The Writers

Two childhood friends, a blond and a redhead, who dreamed of becoming successful writers, practiced their craft whenever they got the chance. Poems, haikus, short stories, plays; you name it, they wrote it. And when one finished a project the other would read it and critique it.

As they got older they attended the same prestigious writing program but the redhead always came second to the blond in competitions and awards. They admired one another and promised to support one another in their careers. However, no matter what the redhead wrote, he never bested the blond.

One day the redhead submitted a horror screenplay to a big Hollywood studio and it was greenlit, cast, and in preproduction within a matter of months. He was so excited that he decided to unfriend everyone on Facebook except for the blond. Off the redhead went to Hollywood, but with promises that he would keep in touch with his friend the blond.

As the blond drove home from dropping his redheaded friend off at the airport, a voice from the radio started to talk to him. The voice sounded like Ralph Cramden, gruff and loud:

"If I were you I'd ask your friend where he got that screenplay from," said the voice.

"Excuse me?" asked the blond.

"That so-called friend of yours stole your story and now they're making a movie of it. A movie *you* should be getting credit for."

"He would never do such a thing," the blond said.

"Oh yeah? Ask him why he never showed you the screenplay when you two share everything you write. Actually, don't ask him, because he'll lie about it. Just check your folders and you'll see there is a missing story."

And so the blond went home. Actually first he got a speeding ticket from a very attractive female officer, and then he nearly hit a man on a Segway. Then he got home and perused his writing folders and lo and behold, one of his manuscripts was missing.

But it was too late. The blond couldn't do anything about

it. He had written the manuscript by hand and he didn't have another copy. There was no way to prove that he was the original author of the screenplay.

Days, weeks, months had passed and he hadn't heard a peep from his friend in Hollywood. Then the redhead sent him a postcard listing all the famous actors and celebrities he had been cavorting with. Coffee with Clooney. Amphetamines with Aniston. Tequila with Tarantino. The name-dropping went on and on. It rubbed the blond the wrong way, and he tore up the postcard.

A year had past and the redhead and the blond hadn't contacted each other. The redhead was too busy gallivanting with his famous friends. They attended his movie premiere, which didn't go over so well, and the redhead found himself alone in the corner of the room at the afterparty. The reviews came out and the film got an F from CinemaScore and a 1 percent on Rotten Tomatoes. From that day on no one in Hollywood would return the redhead's phone calls.

When the redhead moved back home, ashamed and defeated, he ran into the blond at the local 7-11, near the Slurpee machine.

As the redhead approached the blond to apologize, he slipped and cracked his head on the wet, Slurpee-covered floor. He died instantly, cherry-red Slurpee spreading from his head like blood from a gunshot wound.

The blond went on to write a movie about their friendship and gained tremendous success and fame and accolades.

The Dip and the Dish

On the St. Charles Bridge, in the lovely city of Prague, stood a young girl of about 20 years of age named Delilah. She wore a cute little flirty dress and held a folded newspaper in her hand. Near her, at one end of the bridge, a sign warned tourists: *Beware of Pickpockets!* She watched men pass, inconspicuously eyeing their hands. Upon seeing the sign the passersby reflexively checked their pockets to make sure their wallets were still in the right place. Little did they know they were telling Delilah exactly where she needed to dip her deft, flawless fingers.

"The bigger the bulge, the better the pay," her boyfriend Quinn always said.

When she bumped her marks, it was always in a crowd. Her favorite move was called "kissing the dog," a face-to-face encounter, where the wallet was pilfered right from the mark's inner coat pocket. It was freed, rested in the folded newspaper and dropped into Quinn's folded magazine. He was the "dish," the guy she handed off the wallet to, in case the mark got suspicious.

Every night after a successful day of fingersmithing, Delilah and Quinn would unwind at an upscale American-style joint with a bottle of Dream Absinthe. All dips ended their days by calming their nerves with the green fairy. But absinthe had an adverse effect on Quinn. He would raise his glass of absinthe to toast, "To the dip and the dish." But instead of calming him, it riled him up, and at the end of the night Delilah always had a few more bruises on her face and body.

The weeks passed and the emptied wallets filled up the gutters, mailboxes and public trashcans. Delilah had become the city's best dip. No one would be the wiser.

Delilah had trained with Sir Marco in his underground School of Ten Bells—a roomful of suited mannequins with bells sewn onto their pockets that rang when the pickpocket made a false move. No prospective pickpocket ever passed his mannequin practice course without ringing most of the bells. But Delilah had special hands, magic hands. "Hands to ruin a thousand trips," Sir Marco had mused.

But as she stood on the Golden Lane near Prague Castle, looking at a picture of a smiling family that she had found in a random mark's wallet, she wanted out of this life. The sweet, innocent look on the little girl's face in the picture reminded Delilah of herself and the dreams she had at that age. But just then she got a text from Quinn: *Get your ass to the cathedral, a mark just walked in with a huge bulge.*

Delilah entered the crowded cathedral, spotted Quinn kneeling in prayer. When she caught his eye he made the sign of the cross, emphasizing the front right pocket. Then he rose and got into position by the side entrance. Delilah zigzagged through the crowd and inched her way to the mark, who was staring at a stained glass window. Delilah maneuvered against him, dipping her digits into his front right pocket. As she sauntered away, something yanked her back—the wallet was connected to a chain that attached to a belt loop on the mark's pants. He grabbed her by the wrist. She looked for Quinn, but he was already gone.

At first the mark didn't say anything. He just starred at her hands. Never before had Delilah been caught; in anticipation of her arrest, her eyes released salty tears.

"These are the most beautiful hands I have ever seen," the mark finally said. "Hand 6 ½, ring 4, golden cinnamon skin."

"Please, sir, let me go," Delilah said, "I'm so sorry."

"Only if you do me one favor."

She nodded.

"Take my card and call me tomorrow morning. I can make you a lot of money with those hands. Here." He took his wallet back from her and slipped a card into her trembling hand.

That night she found herself alone, losing herself to the green fairy, imagining the life she thought she could have, and staring at the business card between her slender fingers.

Clive Barrington, it said. *Hand Model Agent.*

In the early morning hours, she went home and fell fast asleep. A red-faced Quinn woke her, grabbed her by the hair and threw her to the floor.

"What the hell is this?" he yelled, showing her the business card. "You think you can leave me, is that it?"

"Quinn, I can explain!"

"I thought you'd gotten caught. I was worried sick! But then I find *this*. What the fuck?"

"It's nothing. A man thought I had pretty hands and gave me his card."

"Were you gonna tear it up?"

"Of course."

"Then fucking do it. *Now*."

He handed her the card. She hesitated for a moment and then tore it into bits.

Quinn slapped her to the floor. "You even think about leaving me I'll break each and every one of your fingers."

Days passed and all Delilah could do was keep a lookout for Clive Barrington, hand model agent. But every step she took, Quinn was right behind her, keeping a watchful eye.

More stolen wallets piled up. But this time Delilah didn't discard them. Instead, she stashed them in a pillowcase in Quinn's closet. The two spent the night drinking from a bottle of Dream Absinthe, and as Quinn slept into the afternoon, drooling and snoring, Delilah ventured out to find Clive Barrington.

She eventually found him in the cathedral, at the same stained glass window.

"You never called," Clive said. "So I have come here everyday just in case you showed. These are for you." He handed her a pair of white gloves. "You will have a thousand pairs of these."

Delilah gratefully slipped on the gloves. Nobody ever bought her things.

"There are a few clients I'd like you to meet immediately," Clive Barrington said.

"There's one thing I have to do first. Thank you for the gloves."

Delilah headed straight to the police station and informed an officer about Quinn.

The police stormed his apartment and found the pillowcase containing the massive wallet stash.

Quinn went to jail.

There were a dozen pages torn from magazines and newspapers on the wall of his cell. On each one a hand model displayed a product: a ring, a watch, a bracelet. But his favorite one was smack dab in the middle of the wall collage: slender, flawless fingers with golden cinnamon skin, wrapped around the neck of a bottle of Dream Absinthe, enticing the viewer to fall into the hands of the green fairy.

The Cursed Frog

In the very center of Gifu Prefecture lived a well-to-do family. The father was a very strict man of little outward emotion. He had a wife and three boys. The father owned and ran a very successful business that created fake food displays for restaurants and companies all over the world. He was known as the "the culinary con artist" because his fake food creations had fooled so many people into thinking his plates of plastic delicacies were the real thing. Many had even bitten into the delectable, mouthwatering plastic. A man of few words but many fake dishes, he had spent years training his three boys in the craft, hoping that one day, one of them would be worthy of taking over the family business and carrying on the tradition with honor.

Today was presentation day, a yearly occurrence, when each boy would present a fake five-course meal: the "shokuhin sample," they called it. As the mother and father sat across the empty table, a servant rang a bell, and the first boy, Hibiki, entered. He carried in his tray and placed it on the table. He was nervous but stood up straight and tried not to blink as his father studied the fake meal of steamed rabbit's leg with sour lemon curry, multigrain rice, polenta soup, braised cabbage and fig pudding for dessert.

"What do you think, Father?" asked Hibiki.

"It doesn't make my mouth water," he said.

Hibiki carried himself out of the room, sad and dejected.

The bell rung again and this time a tall, handsome boy entered. His name was Hinata. He had the confidence of a warrior charging into battle against an inferior foe. He presented his shokuhin samples and explained each one as if he were a real chef: roasted carp on a bed of caramelized onions, stuffed peppers and cheesy quinoa zucchini fritters. For dessert, a green tea ice cream atop a poached quince.

The father nodded and the mother smiled. But they did not look at their son.

"What do you think, Father?" asked Hinata.

"My mouth waters slightly," the father said.

"I have never seen such glistening peppers, Hinata," said

the mother. Her husband silenced her with a deathly stare. But Hinata strutted away feeling mighty good about himself.

The servant rang the bell a third time and the youngest boy, Haru, entered to present his fake five-course meal. But he had nothing in his hands. He stood before his father, folded his arms and waited. A long pause simmered in the room as the father glared at Haru.

"What is the meaning of this?" he asked.

"Of what, Katashi?" asked Haru.

The father slammed his hand upon the table.

"One does not call his father by name," he said.

"Haru, explain yourself," said the mother.

"Well, mother, I have been forced to participate in this yearly tradition even though I have no interest in creating fake foods."

"You dishonor me son," the father said menacingly.

The mother laid her hand upon her husband's arm.

"You have nothing to present then?" she asked Haru.

"I do," Haru said. "But not here."

Haru led his baffled mother and his irate father and his two confused brothers out to the guesthouse at the far end of their well-manicured property, past a lush garden pond where one red frog watched the family pass by. But the other frogs seemed to hide from the father. Haru wasn't surprised. Everyone cowered in his father's presence, so why not the frogs?

Before Haru led his family inside the guesthouse, he asked each of them to don an eye mask. They complied, but not without much protest and sighing.

When everyone was inside, Haru asked them to remove their masks. Before them, four figures sat around a round table—four exact replicas of each of them, save for Haru. It was uncanny. They were just like the real thing. If a stranger walked in he wouldn't know which one was the real family until someone moved. Silence and awe filled the sitting room of the guesthouse.

"What do you think, Father?" Haru asked sincerely.

"My mouth is dry," he said, mostly to himself. He had to loosen his tie and hold himself up by gripping the back of the chair before him.

"Why have you done this, Haru?" the mother asked.

"Well, mother, I'd rather have a fake family then the real one I already have."

With that, the father stormed out and the mother, humiliated, followed him.

"You're an idiot, Haru," said Hinata. "A true-blue moron."

"But it's pretty amazing, you have to admit," said Hibiki.

Hinata smacked the back of Hibiki's head to shut him up.

Weeks went by, months, and Haru spent that time with his fake family in the guesthouse. He created more life-size versions of each family member and put them in different rooms, creating scenarios that he believed exemplified the interactions of a real family. Haru spent time with his fake father at the checkers table, beating him every time. Haru had nice conversations about his life with his fake mother, about growing up and spending time with his fake brothers.

Haru had never been happier in all his life.

During work breaks, Haru sat at the edge of the pond and watched the frogs leap and swim around. Sometimes he would have staring contests with them. Until one day, the red frog leaped at his feet and said, "Hello, Haru."

"Hello," said Haru, startled.

"It's me," said the red frog. "Hotaka."

"Uncle Hotaka?" asked Haru. "Can this really be you?"

"Your father has done this to me. When he fired me for making a mistake on that order for fake Marcona almonds. I put a couple of fake cashews in there by accident. All the frogs you see here are employees who once worked for your father and all of us he turned into frogs to suffer here in your family's pond."

"What can I do to help you?

"You can turn us back into people."

"How?"

"Get a sample of your father's blood and drop it into the pond. Then and only then will we frogs return to our human forms."

It was summer now, one of the hottest on record. Haru's father knew this and used it to his advantage. He remembered that he paid for the bills and one of those bills was for the electricity to the guesthouse. This meant that he could shut it off at any time. Which is exactly what he did.

Haru entered the guesthouse the next day and found that his fake family was slowly melting. It was sweltering in the guesthouse and the air conditioning wasn't working. Haru was very concerned. The dog days of summer were upon them and it would only get hotter.

Haru discussed his problem with Hotaka the frog. Hotaka recommended Haru bring in a consultant to see what could be done to keep the guesthouse cool without AC. He knew of a company that could fix the situation, but he would only give up the information if Haru could attest to any progress in getting the frogs back into human form.

"I'm working on it, Uncle Hotaka," said Haru.

"Please don't lie to me, Haru," his uncle said. "I'm a frog who can talk and I can smell that you're lying."

"I am busy with my work."

"And I am busy being a frog. If you want to continue your work, then help us get out of this pond."

So Haru went in the middle of the night to where his father slept and silently crawled up to the corner of his bed holding a sharp needle. But his father was not there! When he turned, his father jumped from the shadows, grabbed Haru, and placed a black hood over his head. Haru was carried down the staircase and into the yard, where he was turned into a blue frog.

As his father approached the pond, the other frogs were ready for him. Sharp bamboo shards rose up from the water. The father did not see this, and as he was tossing his son-turned-frog into the water, he felt a sharp pain at the bottom of his right foot. He fell to the ground in pain as blood ran into the pond.

Suddenly an eruption occurred in the middle of the pond. The water bubbled and Haru and a dozen men and women stood in the pond, the water up to their shins.

"Please don't hurt me," the father said. "I'll do whatever you want."

"Give us our jobs back," said Uncle Hotaka.

And their wish was granted, each with a raise and more vacation days.

The next day was a Saturday and Haru loved Saturdays, always had. They were full of roaming cats and high grass and butterflies. There was a knock at the door and there stood a beauty beyond comprehension. A beauty with one flaw: a port-wine stain shaped like an irregular heart over her left eye. But to Haru she was like all the good things about Saturdays rolled into one.

She showed Haru her card, which had her company logo on it, a sunbeam hitting a solar panel.

"Your uncle sent me," she said.

The woman was called Esme, named after her parent's favorite character in literature. She wasn't surprised when she saw his fake family in the guesthouse living room, slowly melting. She thought it was quite beautiful, and she wished that she had her own fake family to help her deal with things that she couldn't share with her real family.

"Some things shouldn't enter the ears of our parents," she said, "no matter what."

"Yes," agreed Haru. "And therapists are too expensive."

"And a wall has no eyes."

"Most of my friends have their noses in their cell phones," said Haru, excited that he could connect with an actual person so easily. "The world has become one with their machines."

They talked for forty-five minutes before they got around to the reason for Esme's visit. She took out a few sheets of paper that displayed her company's solar panels. She suggested a set up that would fit the guesthouse. Plus it would return him some money after a year or two. But when money was discussed Haru's heart sank. He knew he couldn't possible afford the price.

Esme had an idea.

"I tell you what, Haru," she said. "My father owns this business and I think we can make a deal. I can install one large panel if you create something fake for me."

"What would you like me to create?"

"My neglectful husband."

So after studying a cell phone picture, Haru spent every waking hour constructing a replica of Esme's neglectful husband. During a game of chess he told his fake father all about Esme and the deal they had worked out and how happy that made him. It felt good to express his feelings to his fake father. If only he could do this with his real father.

Haru thought he might try. He went to the edge of the family pond and stared at one yellow frog on a lily pad all alone.

"Hello father," Haru said.

The American Flag Blanket

In the very near future a man of great stature and charisma came to Washington D.C. and everybody adored him more than Jesus, more than Buddha, more than Muhammad, more than Meryl Streep. He was the first elected congressman under the Demublican party. He was a handsome man, tall and brooding, and when he spoke people listened. There was never a negative thing said about him in the papers or on the Internet or on TV. He had a lovely wife and three small children, ages 3, 5, and 7.

One day after one of his televised addresses a woman was watching him from the shadows. She was the politician's makeup artist, and she was quite flirtatious, always smiling, always laughing at the right things. She was remarkable with her brushes and used a special powder, highlighting the politician's features in a way that mesmerized people. He took the makeup artist everywhere he went. Every function, every dinner. She even was there for him when he woke up in the morning. The politician's wife never minded. She liked her and they became friends and would brunch on Sundays and play with their kids. The makeup artist herself did not have kids, but it didn't bother her.

Weeks passed and the politician and the makeup artist found themselves alone in his house. She was cutting up orange slices and some juice flung in her right eye. It stung. The politician grabbed a tissue and dabbed her eye gently. In one swift move he pinched the small orange pulp and removed it from her eye. They locked eyes and knew there was an insane sexual spark between the two. But they couldn't do anything in public or it'd be kaput for the politician and his marriage.

The makeup artist had a Volkswagen SUV with tinted windows, and she would drive a mile away and park and wait for the politician's car to pull up. He'd get in her car and they'd drive all around to find a secluded parking spot. Once they parked, usually by a hedge that blocked the sidewalk from the car, they'd crawl into the back and fondle each other like furious demons. It was so hot and heavy that the windows steamed up. When he was ready he splashed the makeup artist's clavicle with his amazing warm semen. Usually a makeup artist always has tissues around, but that one night she had run out, so she grabbed the nearest thing—an American flag blanket, a 35th birthday present from her mother, which the makeup artist detested for some reason.

On his way home, the politician pulled over and tossed the blanket into a black trash bin on the side of the road near an alley. He quickly got back in the car and headed to Target so he could wash his hands and genitals in the public bathroom. When he got home he sat with his family and had a nice dinner. They talked about climate change and Taylor Swift.

As the weeks rolled by the politician's poll numbers kept rising, and he was screwing the makeup artist any chance he could.

"You have a golden vagina," he said.

On a Tuesday, as the politician was driving home after nailing the makeup artist in the back of her SUV, he noticed a homeless man strutting down the sidewalk—wrapped in a familiar-looking American flag blanket.

"Fuck," he said.

He snapped a picture of the homeless man and sent it to the makeup artist. She responded immediately: *Ugh. LOL. Oh shit. I miss your dick.*

As the months rolled by the politician frequently saw the homeless man wrapped in the cum-stained American flag blanket. Each time the blanket seemed to get dirtier and dirtier. The politician hated it. It ate at him. His DNA was walking around D.C., willy-nilly. If someone got a hold of it and tested it they would know it was the politician's sperm.

The makeup artist tried to calm him down.

Don't worry, she texted. *Even if someone tested the blanket how would they know it was yours if they don't have a sample of your DNA?*

The politician replied, *Someone somewhere will know it was your mother's blanket. They could make the connection.*

And: *I miss your golden V.*

And: *I have to do something about that.*

After a month of planning, the politician made a decision. He would destroy that cum-stained American flag blanket forever. He wasn't going to allow a filthy blanket to jeopardize his access to that golden pussy or his career.

At around midnight on a Saturday the politician told his wife that he had an emergency meeting and she shouldn't wait up for him. She had gotten the kids to bed and was catching up on The Voice.

"Some great singers this year," the politician's wife said.

As the politician prowled D.C. for the homeless man, the makeup artist texted him to ask if he wanted to meet up so she could *swallow that cum*. The politician didn't have time to reply—he had spotted someone in an alley, blind drunk and wrapped in the American flag blanket.

The politician had planned to simply yank the blanket off the homeless man and burn it. Instead he went to the trunk of his car and retrieved a graphite precision putter and used it to madly bash away at the person under the blanket. The politician could now see bloodstains soaking into the filthy blanket. After a few silent moments, after his heavy breaths subsided, he yanked the blanket off to reveal not *the* homeless man but some other homeless man.

Suddenly a policeman blocked the mouth of the alley, gun drawn at the politician standing with a golf club in one hand and a filthy bloody American flag blanket in the other.

At that very moment, the politician's cell phone vibrated. He never got the chance to reach into his pocket and see that the makeup artist had texted again: *I want you inside of me.*

The politician was arrested and charged with murder. The makeup artist's mother recognized the American flag blanket on TV and they found the politician's DNA smeared into the fabric, revealing the affair with his makeup artist.

The politician attempted but failed to hang himself in his jail cell.

All he accomplished was one epic erection. He quickly retrieved the hidden cell phone snuck in by one of the female guards who fancied him. He snapped a pic of his raging peen and sent it to the makeup artist with a message: *Do you miss it?*

The Rager

His car at a dead stop on the 101 freeway, a man honked his horn in a rage. He communicated his fury to all the cars around him with the extra-loud horn that he had installed in his black Range Rover. The man then rolled his window down and screamed "morons!" at any one who could hear him. He turned his car into the left shoulder, an illegal move for sure, but he didn't care. He just wanted to get going. He floored his Range Rover, blasting past all the cars in the far left lane, waving his middle finger as he went past.

He had to stomp on his brakes when he came upon debris in the road. He stormed out of his car in a reignited rage. He followed the debris to three smashed and twisted-up cars. Good Samaritans were helping the crash victims, some of whom were severely injured.

The rageful man didn't care. He went up to one of the victims and yelled at her for causing the traffic, an old lady lying barely conscious and bleeding on the hot pavement. Sirens could be heard in the distance. The road rager finished his tirade and drove off before the ambulances came.

He was just in time for his afternoon hot Vinyasa yoga class in Larchmont.

On his way home, he cut off fifteen Priuses, five BMWs and one brown Tesla. He yelled at the Tesla, "Why would any one get a fucking brown Tesla, you asshole fuck?"

When he finally got home he binge-watched a new Netflix show about morally compromised chefs, then slept peacefully to the rushing of ocean waves emanating from his high-end sound machine from Hammacher Schlemmer.

Just before sleep, he wondered if he would ever meet the right person.

After a breakfast of turkey bacon and a kale tropical smoothie with chia seeds, he got in his black Range Rover and sped to Whole Foods for his weekly grocery shopping. On his way he tailgated a matte black Hummer H2, screaming and honking at it like a maniac. He nearly ran over two children and yelled at them for being stupid.

The rageful man spent five hundred dollars on five bags of organic groceries.

The Valley was hot that day, so he decided to shortcut over the hill. But as he turned off Ventura he found himself behind a slow-moving truck and there was no way around it and there was so much traffic there was no room for a U-turn. The rageful man screamed and yelled.

Tuning his radio to KJazz only made him angrier.

"Fuck you and your motherfucking sax, Kenny G!" he shouted.

It took forever to get over the hill, and on his way down a quiet one-lane street in Beverly Hills, a super-fast white Range Rover almost collided with him. Each driver slammed on their brakes just in time, the Ranger Rovers facing each other, inches apart. They assessed each other for a moment, looking through their windshields. Then the rageful man in the black Range Rover watched the woman in the white Range Rover mouth, *Get the fuck out of the way, douchebag.*

Fuck you, he mouthed in response. *You fucking move.*

He was going to be late for his pottery class but he didn't care. She was already late for her anal bleaching appointment in Sherman Oaks and she didn't care either. So they had to settle this the only way they knew how. At the same time, the woman in the white Range Rover and the man in the black Range Rover floored their accelerators to push the other out the way. Their tires squealed and smoked. They reversed and rammed into each other, once, twice, ten times, luxury vehicles head butting and crunching until smoke appeared from under their hoods. The airbags in both cars deployed and the drivers batted them down and drove at each other again. Finally their cars were dead.

Through all the smoke billowing before their windshields the two ragers stared at each other in anger, until, to their surprise, suddenly they were eye-fucking. Then, with a shared smile, they got out of the cars, walked through the smoke toward one another and embraced.

A month later they moved to New York City where they didn't need cars and got married in a sweaty Bikram Yoga studio.

Two years after that, their anger gone, they got divorced.

The Hoarder

On a quiet street in a decrepit Spanish-style house lived a hoarder and his dozen cats. The hoarder had grown up in this house and over the years collected items, trinkets, papers, trash, countless other things. The house smelled like a garbage dump, and his neighbors considered it an eyesore in their neighborhood of McMansions.

The compulsion had started the day his mother went missing. No one knew what happened to her. Not even the hoarder, who had been visiting his cousin when she disappeared. The hoarder speculated sadly that she had died somewhere by accident or maybe she was drinking tequila in some Mexican village. It made no difference to the hoarder, and he collected whatever had meaning to him throughout those years after his mother's disappearance, which was almost everything.

The neighbors were disgusted by all the trash erupting from his windows and doors. They never saw him, but they could hear when the hoarder moved around the house, because piles of stuff would avalanche out into the yard. The cats dragged various trinkets into the street or left them beneath the parked cars. The neighbors were starting to worry that their street would soon be covered by the hoarder's belongings.

One day a cop visited the hoarder. He could not reach the front door to knock because it was covered in trash. So he used his megaphone to communicate. The hoarder raised his rusty homemade periscope to see who was there. He had made it from a lead pipe and his mother's old hand mirrors. Unfortunately a mountain of debris blocked his view of the front entrance. So he sent messages via his cats.

The first cat appeared out of the trash, and padded up to the cop with a scroll of paper tucked into its collar. The note said, *Hello, can I help you?*

The cop saw Post-it notes and a shaved-down pencil by the mailbox and wrote a message back: *I am a police officer. Your home is in violation of various health and safety codes.*

The cat took the Post-it note in its mouth and disappeared into the debris.

A minute later another cat arrived:

I'm so sorry, officer. But I'd like to be left alone.

The police officer wrote, *I'll be back with someone from the Department of Health and Sanitation.*

The hoarder replied, *Please don't!*

But the officer was gone before he could read the hoarder's note. The hoarder began to panic, fearing that his accumulated treasures might soon be gone. He hid in his room under a heap of National Geographic magazines and Chinese food take-out boxes. His cats cuddled with him.

Days later the cop escorted an inspector from the Health Department to the hoarder's home. The police officer had instructed him in how to communicate with the hoarder. When a cat appeared, the inspector tucked a message into its collar:

Hello, sir, I've come to inspect your home, is there any way inside?

The hoarder wrote back: *No, unfortunately not. Please go away!*

The supervisor wrote: *This house is a health risk to the neighborhood. I will return with a cleaning crew next Tuesday between 8am-11am.*

The hoarder wrote: *I don't consent to this. Leave me alone!*

He was so terrified that he barricaded each door of his house with piles of soiled clothes. Then he burrowed as deep as he could go below a years worth of pizza boxes and old newspapers.

In the days before the official cleanup, the hoarder's cats began a herculean task. At first it seemed that his cats were digging random tunnels through the hoardings. He could hear them working their way back and forth, dropping small items on the front porch. Items the hoarder couldn't see with his lead-pipe periscope. As the days went by it sounded like the cats were bringing up larger and larger items.

He fixed his periscope at his neighbors watching with disapproval from their front lawns, their faces twisted in horror and disgust. This didn't look good for the hoarder.

On the appointed day, the cop, the inspector and a cleanup crew arrived. There was so much crap that nobody noticed the piles of items that the cats had neatly arranged from small to large on the front porch. The workers started the enormous job. A dump truck arrived and a small digger rolled up to collect the outpouring of trash. Firemen came and freed the hoarder from his seclusion. When he stumbled onto his neglected lawn, the neighbors saw a morbidly obese man, not the skinny gentleman they remembered. He looked like he hadn't seen the sun in years and his skin was ashen and pale. He called for his cats but they didn't come.

It was then when the hoarder noticed the items his cats had arranged on his porch. They were bones.

Just then a worker emerged from the house, babbling something about clearing out the basement and finding *this*: a human skull.

Which was when everybody else noticed the neat piles of bones.

After a short investigation, the coroner concluded that the skull had belonged to a middle-aged woman, who, 30 years earlier, had likely died of blunt force trauma to the head. The coroner believed that the dent in the skull suggested a metal pipe of some sort, but nobody would ever know for sure.

The Editor

In a small studio apartment on the Upper East Side of Manhattan an editor sat staring at a pile of five unsolicited manuscripts. She knew deep down in her heart that they were all going to be clunkers. Finding a good book in this pile would be harder than winning the Mega Millions jackpot. The memory of when she had been a struggling writer, hoping for that one chance to show the world her talents, had died long ago. But now, although she dreaded the slush pile, she did relish her role as a cruel god holding the fate of these writers in her hands.

She had a foolproof method: if she liked the title, she'd read the first page. If she liked the first page she'd read the first ten, then the first thirty. After that, which only happened once, maybe twice a year, she'd finish the entire manuscript in one sitting.

The impossible happened. She finished each and every book. This baffled her and so the following day she read each submission for a second time. She thought maybe something was wrong with her, so she had her assistants read the books, which all passed with very high marks. Even her Cuban doorman who had only ever read one book his whole life, a Choose Your Own Adventure called *Who Killed Harlowe Thwomby?*—even he couldn't put the manuscripts down.

The editor was so mystified that she called each writer into her office at the same time and asked them one question: What is the best hamburger in New York City?

This confused all the writers. Was this a trick of some kind? If they answered wrong would it mean that they would never see their beloved work in a bookstore?

It was a real question. Each writer had to accompany the editor's ten-year-old nephew, Benji, as he tried the place that they believed had the best burger. Benji never smiled, never said thank you and never shared a cab with any of them. He preferred to walk, and he went straight to his aunt's place to tell her that he didn't like any of the hamburgers.

So the editor called the writers back into her office to ask them another question: What is your favorite Broadway show? So they each found themselves escorting little Benji to a show. After curtain call, Benji would pick out whatever souvenir he wanted. Then he'd call up his aunt to tell her that he had hated every show, even *Hamilton: The Musical*.

The editor was at her wit's end. She called the writers back in to ask one final question: Am I beautiful?

All the writers but one said yes. So she decided to publish that one writer's manuscript, because he had told the truth. But there was one condition: that ten-year-old Benji would be allowed to make whatever changes he liked to the story.

This infuriated the winning writer. Benji didn't even have good taste: the writer had loved *Hamilton: The Musical*.

Then the writer, pacing in his own small Brooklyn apartment, had an epiphany. He decided to pull his manuscript from the editor and publish it himself.

So after months of research he formed a corporation and called the other four rejected writers and told them he'd like to publish their books. They all happily agreed.

The next year all five of their books reached the New York Times Best Seller list. His publishing company, Benji Sucks LLC, went on to become the foremost publisher of wrongly rejected books.

The Time Capsule

It was the end of days. Climate change had devastated countries worldwide. Population had dwindled to very low numbers. Humans had failed.

In an effort to preserve some idea of mankind, a dying scientist and his young daughter Imani had decided to put all their efforts into creating a time capsule that would hold one item to be locked, lowered, and sealed in an underground vault. That item would represent mankind to any future generations or extraterrestrials that might discover it. Imani led the effort and sent out a signal to the far corners of what was left of the world: anyone who reached the arena by a certain date was invited to submit their idea for one item that would represent the essence of mankind.

Imani's father never got to see the ideas. Imani had taken care of him the best she could, but the sickness and pain became too much to bear for the both of them. On the last night of his life, before bed, she washed him and held his hand. As he fell asleep, Imani promised she would choose a worthy offering for the time capsule. Through tears, Imani placed a pillow over his face and ended his suffering.

After his death, Imani buried him in sacred ground. She painted the time capsule with a name that would forever honor her father: *Jabari's Capsule*. And then she waited. She spent her time making jars of mulled wine and staying in top physical condition by carrying jugs of water up a hill. She watched old movies on VHS and studied self-defense videos from a defunct YouTube archive.

Imani had turned a nearby field into a makeshift arena and soon it was occupied with a handful of participants from around the world. Eight to be exact, not including Imani, who instructed them to display their offerings on a table by the time capsule. Imani placed a countdown clock on the table. She pressed a button and digital numbers appeared. Imani announced that each participant would approach their item, reveal it, and within five minutes explain the reasoning behind their offering.

"What is the meaning of this?" someone asked. "Five

minutes? We came all this way, some of us across vast bodies of water, and this is all the time we get to explain ourselves?"

"He's right!" the other seven roared in protest.

"Calm down everyone!" Imani said. "If we have all the time in the world, we will never agree on anything, and my father's efforts will be in vain."

Muttering, the participants returned to their seats. First up was a man from the Far East. He opened a small ornate chest to reveal an intricately folded origami butterfly. The man held the butterfly in his hands and deftly unfolded it, revealing hundreds of mathematical equations. He walked it around the makeshift arena so the others could see. The curious participants leaned in to get a better look at the surprise the butterfly kept in its folds.

"The most famous and beautiful equations that man has devised can be found on the wings of this butterfly," said the man from the Far East. "This is how we will demonstrate the capability of the human mind and its impact on existence. Thank you!"

Imani smiled, wishing her father could see such a beautiful thing.

A pompous man in a tweed suit and spectacles approached the table and lifted up a sharpened pencil. "Man cannot produce those equations without the tool of the writer. And what an important weapon to wield. I challenge any of you to best this tool of man." He took a seat and crossed his arms. No one liked the writer.

Two Australian women approached the table, hand in hand, and lifted a book with a golden cross inlaid on a leather-bound cover. "God created the heavens and the Earth and sent his son to save us from ourselves. It's all here. And we believe that if an alien species or anyone not of this Earth were to find this, they'd truly understand who we are. God bless you!"

The pompous writer scoffed. "Please. Where was your god when the whole world was going to hell, huh?"

"Okay, we are not here to judge," Imani said. "Who's next?"

An American farmer humbly walked to the table and removed a sheet to reveal his offering — a wooden wheel. He didn't say anything. The wheel spoke for itself. Everyone was impressed and knew it would be hard to beat.

A teenaged girl from Canada reached the table and pointed to a cellphone. "This was the last, and in my opinion, the best model of a cellphone to ever be created. On it is every song, every book, every movie, every newspaper article created by earthlings. This shows and reveals what we are about. A pencil is only as effective as the mind that wields it. Some smart person said that I think. A wheel is cool I guess, but it's so primitive."

"Thank you for your offering," Imani said. "But how would future species know how to turn it on?"

"Just because I'm sixteen doesn't mean I'm stupid," the Canadian girl said. "Duh!" She snaked a phone charger from her backpack and slammed it on the table next to the phone. "I believe I'm winning now!"

Imani was aware that wasn't an answer to her specific question. But she figured there was no reason to point out the obvious. She called for a lunch break. The men and women from around the globe noshed on a delicacy brought by one of the participants: Spam. They had dubbed it "Apocalypse Chow," savoring each necessary bite of the canned cooked meat, while sipping the mulled wine made by Imani. As they ate, the participants debated the items; and although some admired the wheel and the origami butterfly, the cellphone seemed to be the frontrunner.

Feeling resentful an misunderstood, the writer rushed to the table, and in a flash of anger, snapped his pencil in two.

When the contest reconvened, a lanky dude from California meandered to the table. It didn't seem like he remembered where his item was located. He used up most of his five minutes trying to find it. When he laid eyes on his hemp satchel he smiled. He took out a multi-compartment container.

"Dudes! I give you the Earth's greatest natural gift. It heals, it helps, it makes us laugh. You can smoke it, vape it, eat it, drink it and wear it. In my container are the seeds of all the major strains, Sativa and Indica. Cannabis my friends! Peace!"

The dude from California sat down, pleased with himself.

Imani thought, "He is high as a kite."

Next was a man from Budapest with a distant stare. He approached the table and silently stood there for a full minute.

"And what is your offering, sir?" Imani asked.

"I offer nothing," he said.

"Nothing?"

"That is correct. For we do not deserve to be remembered."

"Why do you think that?" Imani said, trying not to roll her eyes.

"We have destroyed and squandered every good thing we've inherited or created. The warning from scientists such as your father were ignored. So I believe that we should put nothing in the time capsule. Nothing is my offering."

When he walked back to his seat all eyes were on him. Imani had an eerie feeling. Maybe he was right?

"Well, thank you for your offering, sir," was all she could muster. "Who is next?"

They all looked around and realized that everyone had had their say.

"Well then, my father and I would like to close this contest with our own offering."

She took out three vials from an impact-resistant briefcase. "I give you samples of human blood. One of mine and one of my father's. The third vial contains a swab of my DNA. So much can be deduced and learned about human beings studying these three samples. My father Jabari always said that everything we need to learn about homo sapiens can be found inside of us."

She closed the case and secured its contents.

Imani now reset the countdown clock for a sixty-minute debate. As the participants respectfully listened to each other's arguments and recommendations, no one noticed the dashing cowboy standing at the entrance of the arena, wielding a small handgun.

"Sorry I'm late, ya'll," he said, heading for the table. He perused the offerings and snickered at what he saw. "Are ya'll serious right now? This is what you think represents the best of mankind? I highly doubt that some extra-tie-restrial is gonna learn anything from these here items."

"Sorry sir," Imani said. "The contest is closed."

"Closed? Now come on people. I've brought the very best invention that mankind has ever devised. This here M1911 pistol produced by John Browning is a masterpiece of form and function. Where shall I put it? Can I just place it here?"

Without waiting for an answer, he twirled the pistol like a gunslinger and then placed it next to the broken pencil.

A debate erupted about the merits of a gun. Suddenly that was all everybody could talk about. It angered them, made them anxious. It reminded Imani of violence and suffering. Others were reminded of victory and safety and responsibility.

At the twenty-minute mark, Imani interrupted the participants.

"Our time is almost up," she said. "We need to make a decision."

Imani passed out squares of paper and a pencil to each participant.

"Mark your top three choices," she said.

"See?" the writer told everyone. "You see how important pencils are?"

Imani watched the seconds tick away on the clock as the participants concentrated on their choices. At the five-minute mark, the man from Budapest with the distant stare stumbled to the table to look over the offerings. He reached for his stomach and fell to the ground. A red froth oozed out of his mouth. No one had time to run to him as each participant began to retch up red liquid and drop to their deaths. Imani watched in horror. There were two minutes left on the clock and the only one left standing was Imani. Or so she thought.

"Hi!"

Imani yelped as she turned to face the voice that startled her. It was the cowboy, standing unharmed at the outskirts of the arena. He grinned at the scattered bodies.

"But why didn't you drink the wine?" he asked Imani.

"You? You did this?" Imani asked, terrified. "But how?"

"Well you see, before these here good people arrived I was already on your property," the cowboy explained. "I waited until you carried your water jugs up that there hill and emptied my special powder into your mulled wine."

"But why?" Imani asked. "What did these people ever do to you?"

"We're all gonna die shortly," he said. "Why should we suffer any longer? Besides, I want my gun to be the winner."

The minute mark arrived and a chamber in the ground, below the time capsule, began to open.

Time was running out for Imani's contest.

Imani and the cowboy ran for the items on the table, slamming into one another, causing the table to tip over. Imani crawled away as the cowboy reached for the broken pencil. He tried to jab Imani in the neck but she blocked it with the surprisingly thick paper of the origami butterfly. The cowboy found the cellphone charger and wrapped it around Imani's throat. Losing oxygen quickly, Imani writhed and managed to get her ankle over the spoke of the wooden wheel. She scooped up the wheel with her foot and grabbed ahold of it, slamming it down into the cowboy's face. He went reeling back, tripping over the hemp satchel bag. As he lay there Imani walked over to him and poured the vials of blood into his eyes, temporarily blinding him.

"This contest is over!," said Imani, trying to catch her breath. "I win!" She grabbed the heavy countdown clock and as she was lifting it over her head the cowboy pointed something at her. The gun.

"You lose," he said.

The explosion of the gunshot drowned out the crushing thud the clock made against his head.

The bullet had pierced Imani's belly. She keeled over, dropping to her hands and knees. The cowboy was already dead.

The damaged clock had ten seconds remaining as her blood dripped out onto the Earth.

Imani was losing consciousness. Her eyes locked onto something resting on the ground. She knew she would break that promise to her father. But something was better than nothing.

Spam.

"I am so sorry father," were her last words.

As her life came to a bloody end, she grabbed the

remaining canned meat, crawled to Jabari's capsule, tossed the Spam inside, and the doors shut forever.

About the Author

Jason Antoon does a lot of stuff. Primarily an actor, he graduated with debt from the prestigious acting program at Carnegie Mellon University. His big acting break came in the 2000 Tony Award-winning Broadway musical *Contact*, which garnered him a Drama Desk Nomination for Best Supporting Actor in a Musical.

Since then he's worked in countless film and TV projects, from Steven Spielberg's *Minority Report* to TNT's award-winning dramedy *Claws*.

He created and starred in two acclaimed web series: *Vamped Out* and *Bitter Party of 5*. He lives in Los Angeles with his wife and two children.

This is his first work of fiction.

For more info go to JasonAntoon.com.

About Dutch Kills Press

Dutch Kills Press is dedicated to eradicating the idea of writing for exposure. Each contributor earns fifty percent of the profit from his or her book, period.

Our intention is to marry the editorial expertise of traditional publishing with the speed and ease of the digital world, and, in doing so, help creative people generate income.

Please have a look at DutchKillsPress.com, where you can peruse more of our interesting and inexpensive books.

CPSIA information can be obtained
at www.ICGtesting.com
Printed in the USA
LVHW08s1224300918
591917LV00024B/1543/P